ACKNOWLEDGEMENTS

A very merry "thank you" to my friends and members of my family
who posed for the characters found throughout this edition of
A Christmas Treasury.

CAST OF CHARACTERS

Michael Paglia - Santa
Dena Hansen - Mary
Adam Kubert - Joseph
Joseph Scrocco, Jr. - Shepherd
William McGuire - Shepherd
Greg Hildebrandt - Shepherd, King, Sailor
Kevin McGinty - Angel
Alicia DeVincenzi - Child Caroling
Jim McCann - Child Caroling
Heidi Corso - Angel
Vincent Colandrea - Medieval Lord
Jean Scrocco - Medieval Lady
Ron Maiver - Squire
Honey Maiver - Lady In Waiting
Gene O'Brien - King, Papa ('Twas)
Linda Hanover - Young Lover
Alan Hallerman - Young Lover
Gregory Hildebrandt - Elf
Karen White - Elf
Robbie McCann - Child Sleeping
Annie Green - Child Sleeping

A Christmas Treasury

Illustrated by

Greg Hildebrandt

The Unicorn Publishing House
New Jersey

The Unicorn Publishing House; 1148 Parsippany Blvd.; Parsippany, NJ 07054

Distributed in Canada by Doubleday Canada, Ltd., Toronto, ON, Canada
Distributed in the rest of the world by Columbus Books, Ltd., London, England

◆◆◆◆◆

Designed and Edited by Jean L. Scrocco
Music consultant: Dale Trimmer
Printed in the United States of America by R.R. Donnelley & Sons, New York, NY
Typography by TG&IF, Inc., Fairfield, NJ
Reproduction photography by The Color Wheel, New York, NY
Color Separations by Compucolor, Morristown, NJ

◆◆◆◆◆

Special thanks to Kate Klimo

◆◆◆◆◆

Printing History 15 14 13 12 11 10 9 8 7 6 5 4 3 2 1

Library of Congress Cataloging in Publication Data
Main entry under title:

A Christmas Treasury.

Summary: Includes illustrated versions of eight carols,
the story of the Nativity, and the famous narrative
poem about St. Nicholas' Christmas Eve Visit.

1. Christmas — Literary collections. [1. Christmas —
Literary collections] I. Hildebrandt, Greg, ill.
PZ5.C476 1984349.2'6828284-8798
ISBN 0-88101-013-8.

'Twas The Night Before Christmas

By
C. Clement Moore

'Twas the night before Christmas,
When all through the house,
Not a creature was stirring, not even a mouse.

The stockings were hung by the chimney with care,
In hopes that St. Nicholas soon would be there.

The children were nestled all snug in their beds,
While visions of sugarplums danced in their heads.

And Mamma in her kerchief, and I in my cap,
Had just settled down for a long winter's nap.

When out on the lawn there arose such a clatter,
I sprang from my bed to see what was the matter.

Away to the window I flew like a flash,
Tore open the shutters and threw up the sash.

The moon on the breast of the new-fallen snow,
Gave a luster of midday to objects below,

When, what to my wondering eyes should appear,
But a miniature sleigh, and eight tiny reindeer,
With a little old driver, so lively and quick,
I knew in a moment it must be St. Nick.

More rapid than eagles his coursers they came,
And he whistled, and shouted, and called them by name:,

"Now, Dasher! Now, Dancer! Now, Prancer and Vixen!
On, Comet! On, Cupid! On, Donder and Blitzen!
To the top of the porch! To the top of the wall!
Now, dash away! Dash away! Dash away all!"

As dry leaves that before the wild hurricane fly,
When they meet with an obstacle, mount to the sky,
So up to the housetop the coursers they flew,
With the sleigh full of toys, and St. Nicholas, too.

And then in a twinkling, I heard on the roof
The prancing and pawing of each little hoof.

As I drew in my head, and was turning around,
Down the chimney St. Nicholas came with a bound.

He was dressed all in fur, from his head to his foot,
And his clothes were all tarnished with ashes and soot.
A bundle of toys he had flung on his back,
And he looked like a peddler just opening his pack.

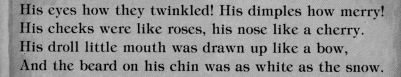

His eyes how they twinkled! His dimples how merry!
His cheeks were like roses, his nose like a cherry.
His droll little mouth was drawn up like a bow,
And the beard on his chin was as white as the snow.

The stump of a pipe he held tight in his teeth,
And the smoke, it encircled his head like a wreath.
He had a broad face and a little round belly,
That shook, when he laughed, like a bowl full of jelly.

He was chubby and plump, a right jolly old elf,
And I laughed when I saw him, in spite of myself.
A wink of his eye and a twist of his head,
Soon gave me to know I had nothing to dread.

He spoke not a word, but went straight to his work,
And filled all the stockings, then turned with a jerk,
And laying his finger aside of his nose,
And giving a nod, up the chimney he rose.

He sprang to his sleigh, to his team gave a whistle,
And away they all flew like the down of a thistle.

But I heard him exclaim as he drove out of sight,
"Happy Christmas to all, and to all a good night."

The Nativity of Jesus

In those days Caesar Augustus
published a decree ordering a
census of the whole world. This
first census took place while
Quirinius was governor of Syria.

Everyone went to register, each to
his own town. And so Joseph
went from the town of Nazareth
in Galilee to Judea, to David's
town of Bethlehem - because he
was of the house and lineage of
David - to register with Mary, his
espoused wife, who was with
child.

While they were there the days of her confinement were completed.

She gave birth to her first-born son and wrapped him in swaddling clothes and laid him in a manger, because there was no room for them in the place where travelers lodged.

There were shepherds in that locality, living in the fields and keeping night watch by turns over their flocks. The angel of the Lord appeared to them as the glory of the Lord shone around them, and they were very much afraid. The angel said to them: "You have nothing to fear! I come to proclaim good news to you - tidings of great joy to be shared by the whole people. This day in David's city a savior has been born to you, the Messiah and Lord. Let this be a sign to you: in a manger you will find an infant wrapped in swaddling clothes." Suddenly, there was with the angel a multitude of the heavenly host, praising God and saying,

"Glory to God in high heaven, peace on earth to those on whom his favor rests."

When the angels had returned to heaven, the shepherds said to one another: "Let us go over to Bethlehem and see this event which the Lord has made known to us." They went in haste and found Mary and Joseph, and the baby lying in the manger; once they saw, they understood what had been told them concerning this child. All who heard of it were astonished at the report given them by the shepherds.

Mary treasured all these things and reflected on them in her heart. The shepherds returned, glorifying and praising God for all they had heard and seen, in accord with what had been told them.

"Glory to God in high heaven,
peace on earth to those on
whom his favor rests."

Carols And Songs

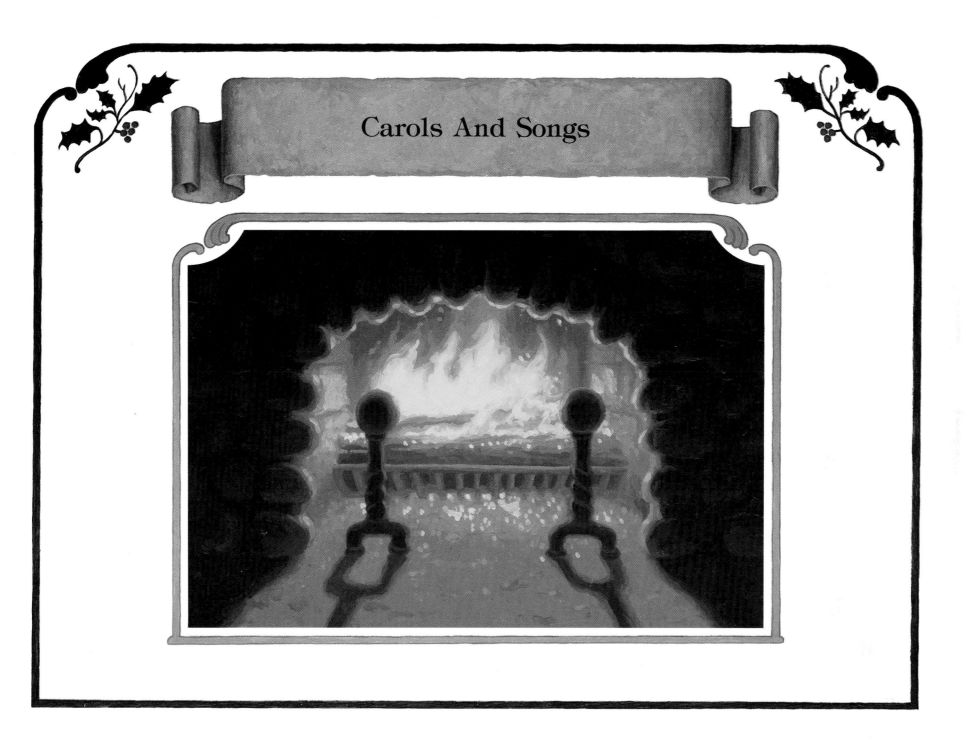

Silent Night

I Saw Three Ships

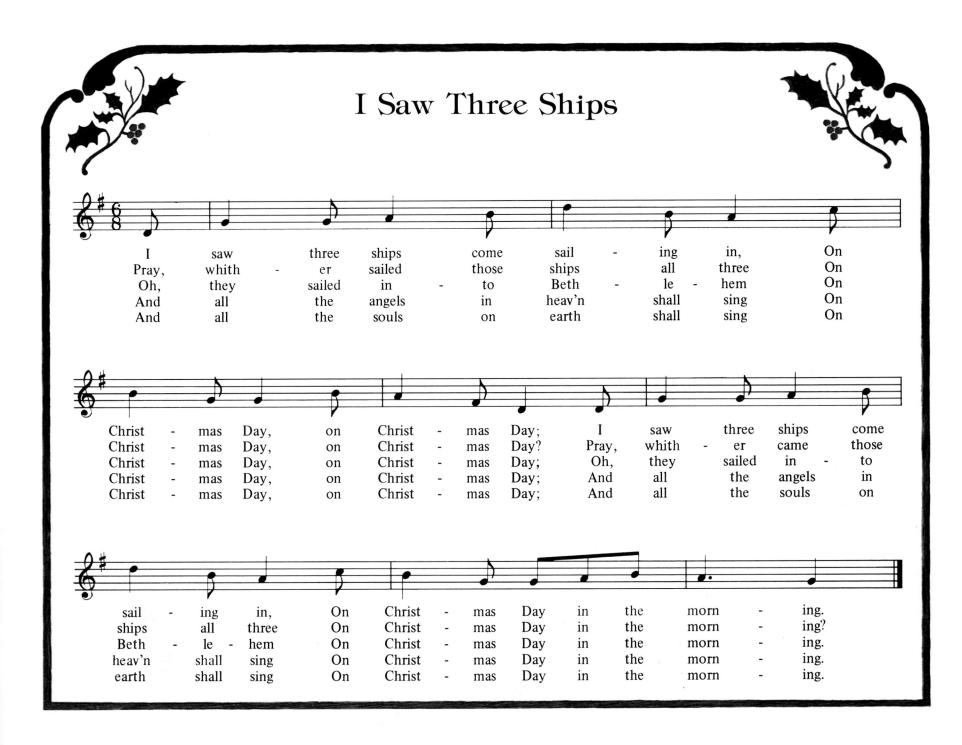

Deck The Halls

Deck   the halls with boughs of hol - ly,   Fa - la - la - la - la,   la - la - la - la;
See   the blaz - ing yule be - fore us,
Fast   a - way the old year pass - es,

'Tis   the sea - son to be jol - ly,   Fa - la - la - la - la,   la - la - la - la.
Strike the harp and join the cho - rus,
Hail   the new, ye lads and lass - es,

Don   we now our gay ap - par - el,   Fa - la - la, fa - la - la, la - la - la.
Fol - low me in mer - ry mea - sure,
Sing   we joy - ous songs to - geth - er,

Troll   the an - cient Christ - mas car - ol,   Fa - la - la - la - la,   la - la - la - la.
While I tell of Christ - mas trea - sure,
Head - less of the wind and weath - er,

Jingle Bells

It Came Upon The Midnight Clear

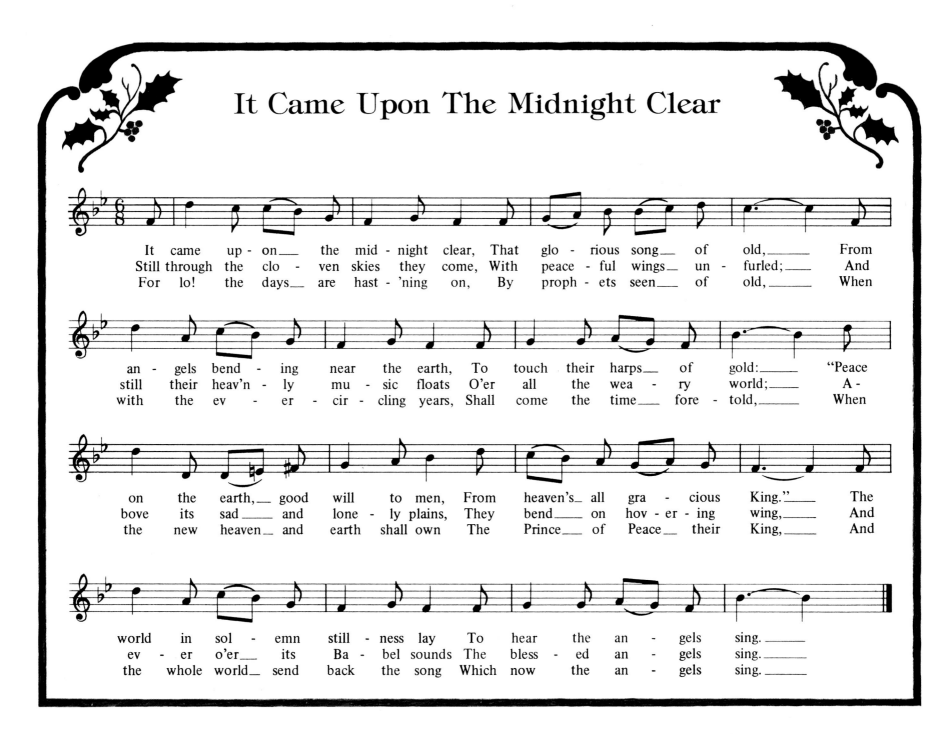

It came up - on the mid - night clear, That glo - rious song of old,   From
Still through the clo - ven skies they come, With peace - ful wings un - furled;   And
For lo! the days are hast - 'ning on, By proph - ets seen of old,   When

an - gels bend - ing near the earth, To touch their harps of gold: "Peace
still their heav'n - ly mu - sic floats O'er all the wea - ry world;   A -
with the ev - er - cir - cling years, Shall come the time fore - told,   When

on the earth, good will to men, From heaven's all gra - cious King."   The
bove its sad and lone - ly plains, They bend on hov - er - ing wing,   And
the new heaven and earth shall own The Prince of Peace their King,   And

world in sol - emn still - ness lay To hear the an - gels sing.
ev - er o'er its Ba - bel sounds The bless - ed an - gels sing.
the whole world send back the song Which now the an - gels sing.

O Christmas Tree

We Three Kings

We three kings of O - ri - ent are; Bear - ing gifts we trav - erse a -
Born a King on Beth - le - hem plain, Gold we bring to crown Him a -

far, Field and foun - tain, moor and moun - tain, Fol - low - ing yon - der star.
gain, King for - ev - er, ceas - ing nev - er O - ver us all to reign.

O, _____ star of won - der, star of night, Star with roy - al beau - ty bright;

West - ward lead - ing, still pro - ceed - ing, Guide us to Thy per - fect light.

Twelve Days of Christmas

On the first day of Christmas my true love sent to me
A partridge in a pear tree.

On the second day of Christmas my true love sent to me
Two turtle doves and a partridge in a pear tree.

On the third day of Christmas my true love sent to me
Three French hens,
Two turtle doves and a partridge in a pear tree.

On the fourth day of Christmas my true love sent to me
Four cawing birds, three French hens,
Two turtle doves and a partridge in a pear tree.

On the fifth day of Christmas my true love sent to me
Five gold rings!
Four cawing birds, three French hens,
Two turtle doves and a partridge in a pear tree.

On the sixth day of Christmas my true love sent to me
Six geese a-laying,
Five gold rings!
Four cawing birds, three French hens,
Two turtle doves and a partridge in a pear tree.

On the seventh day of Christmas my true love sent to me
Seven swans a-swimming, six geese a-laying,
Five gold rings!
Four cawing birds, three French hens,
Two turtle doves and a partridge in a pear tree.

On the eighth day of Christmas my true love sent to me
Eight maids a-milking,
Seven swans a-swimming, six geese a-laying,
Five gold rings!
Four cawing birds, three French hens,
Two turtle doves and a partridge in a pear tree.

On the ninth day of Christmas my true love sent to me
Nine ladies dancing, eight maids a-milking,
Seven swans a-swimming, six geese a-laying,
Five gold rings!
Four cawing birds, three French hens,
Two turtle doves and a partridge in a pear tree.

On the tenth day of Christmas my true love sent to me
Ten lords a-leaping,
Nine ladies dancing, eight maids a-milking,
Seven swans a-swimming, six geese a-laying,
Five gold rings!
Four cawing birds, three French hens,
Two turtle doves and a partridge in a pear tree.

On the eleventh day of Christmas my true love sent to me
Eleven pipers piping, ten lords a-leaping,
Nine ladies dancing, eight maids a-milking,
Seven swans a-swimming, six geese a-laying,
Five gold rings!
Four cawing birds, three French hens,
Two turtle doves and a partridge in a pear tree.

On the twelfth day of Christmas my true love sent to me
Twelve drummers drumming,
Eleven pipers piping, ten lords a-leaping,
Nine ladies dancing, eight maids a-milking,
Seven swans a-swimming, six geese a-laying,
Five gold rings!
Four cawing birds, three French hens,
Two turtle doves,
And a partridge in a pear tree!